TEXT BY MARY B. PALMER   PICTURES BY ABNER GRABOFF

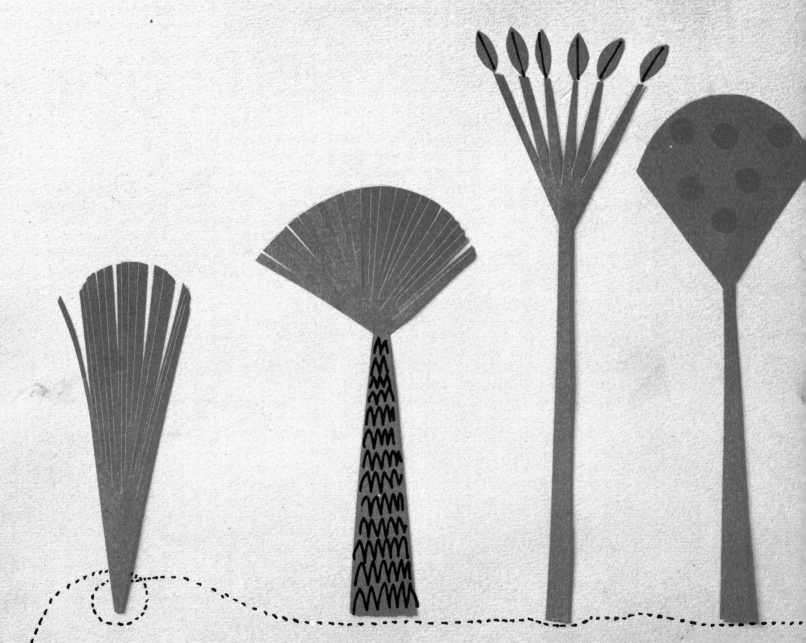

THE NO·SORT·OF·ANIMAL

HOUGHTON MIFFLIN COMPANY BOSTON 1964 THE RIVERSIDE PRESS CAMBRIDGE

To CINDY and BOB

Once there was an animal who was a

No-Sort-of-Animal.

He had everything he needed like

four legs and two eyes and two ears.

But he didn't like being a No-Sort-of-Animal.

He felt very plain.

He wished he could be something else.

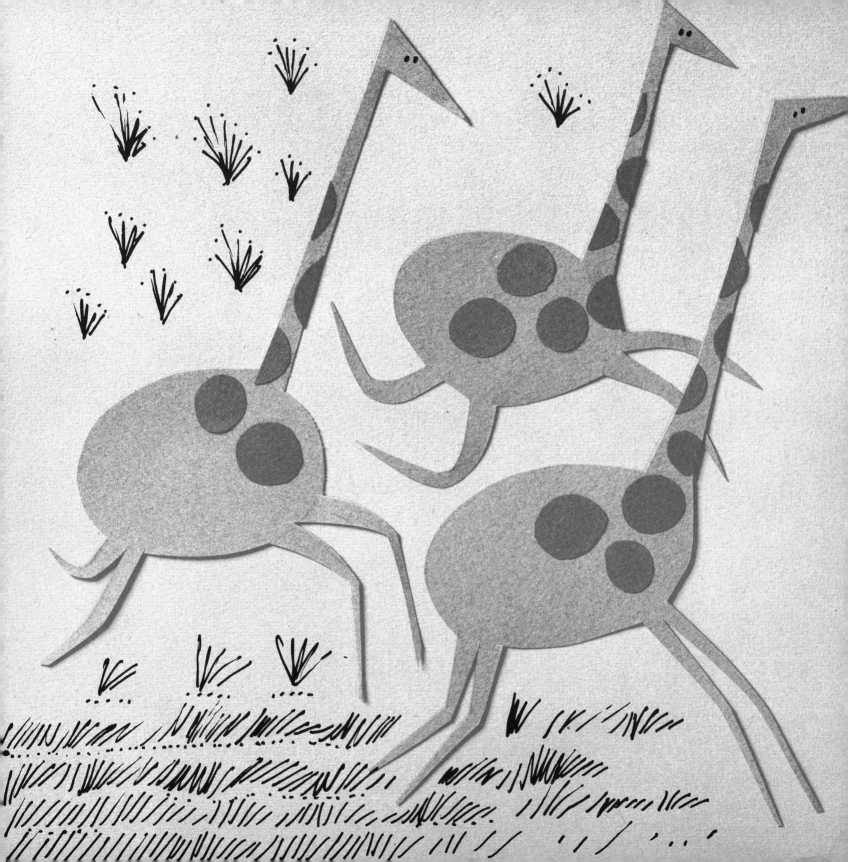

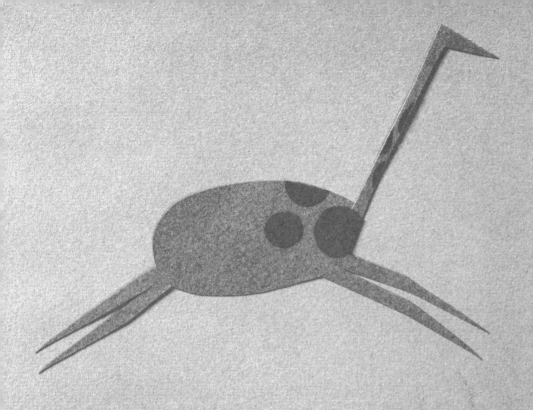

One day he was sitting thinking how plain he was,

when he heard a great clatter of hoofs,

and out of the forest came a herd of giraffes with

beautiful long, graceful necks.

They galloped by the No-Sort-of-Animal

and were out of sight in no time.

"Oh!" he said to himself. "How handsome and distinguished

they are! Why can't *I* look like that?"

So he went to see the
lion, King of all
animals.
"I am so very plain,"
the No-Sort-of-Animal
told the lion.
"Couldn't I have
something more
distinguished like the
Giraffe's neck?"
The lion thought
a minute.
Then he said,
"Yes, I will arrange
that."

And it was arranged

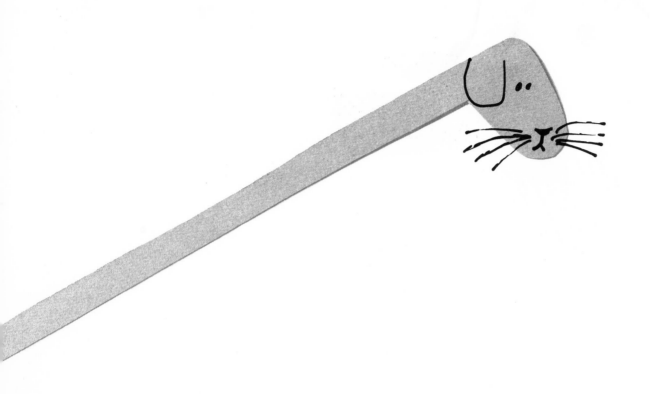

LIKE THIS...

The No-Sort-of-Animal

was very pleased

and proud.

He went skipping off

into the forest.

But he couldn't gallop

like the giraffes

because his legs

were much too short.

And when it came time

to have his lunch,

he had the greatest

difficulty eating.

He never could tell

where his plate was.

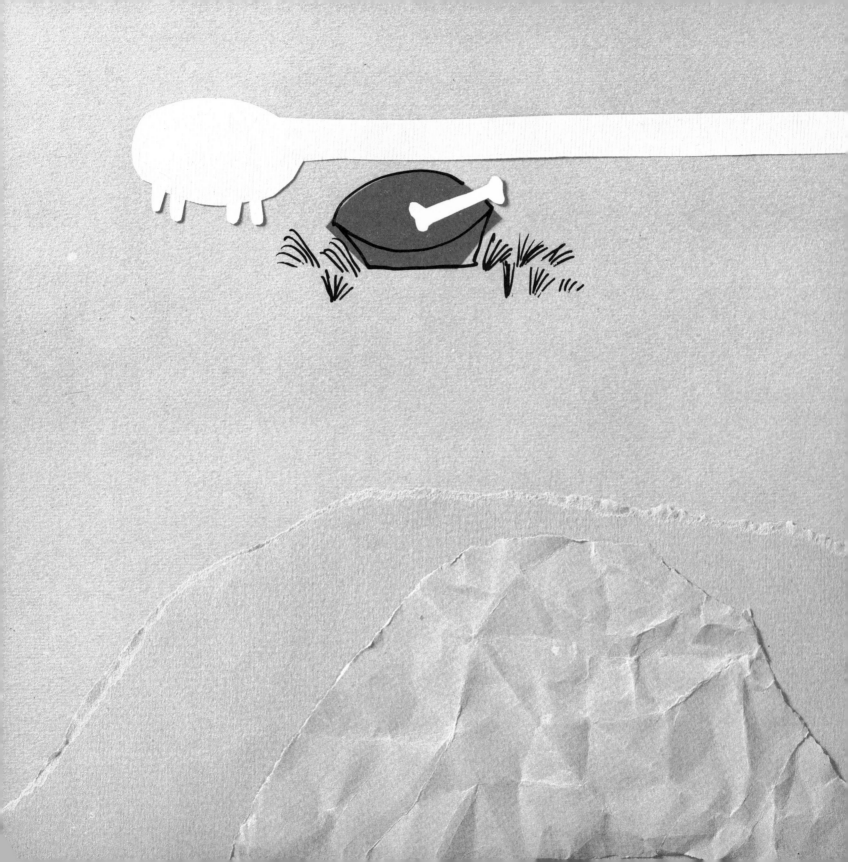

Sometimes he guessed
too far away
and sometimes he guessed
too nearby.

The neck that had looked
so graceful on the
giraffes didn't really
look well at all on him.
He couldn't get used to it.
Everywhere he went
he got all wound up in
trees
and
vines

and at night his neck felt so heavy that he had to build

a special little neck rest.

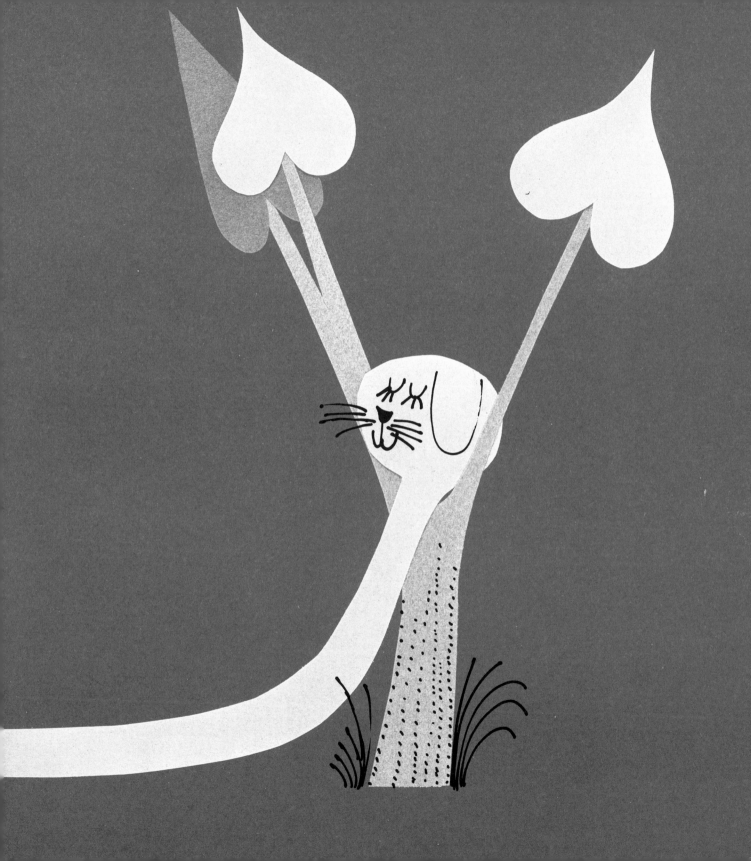

In the middle of the night he was wakened by a great shuffling and thumping, and a herd of elephants came lumbering by in the moonlight.

They were twirling and untwirling their trunks as they passed him on their way to the water hole. The No-Sort-of-Animal watched them drinking water and playfully spraying one another with their trunks.

Just before they left, one of them let out a great trumpeting noise that echoed through the forest.

"How marvelous!" exclaimed the No-Sort-of-Animal.

"How wonderful it would be to have a trunk!"

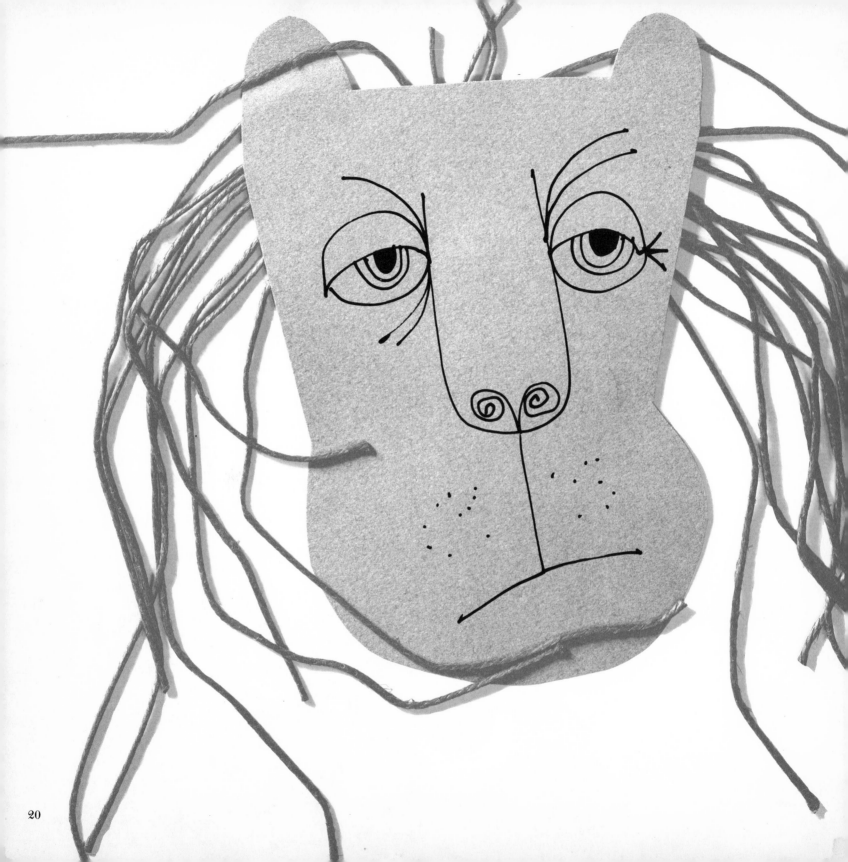

Next day, he went back to see the lion.

"Please," he said to the lion, "I don't want a neck like a giraffe after all."

"Oh *don't* you," the lion said crossly.

"No, what I *really* want is a nice distinguished trunk like an elephant."

"You're a changeable sort of a No-Sort-of-Animal," the lion roared.

But he arranged it anyway,

L I K E

T H I S

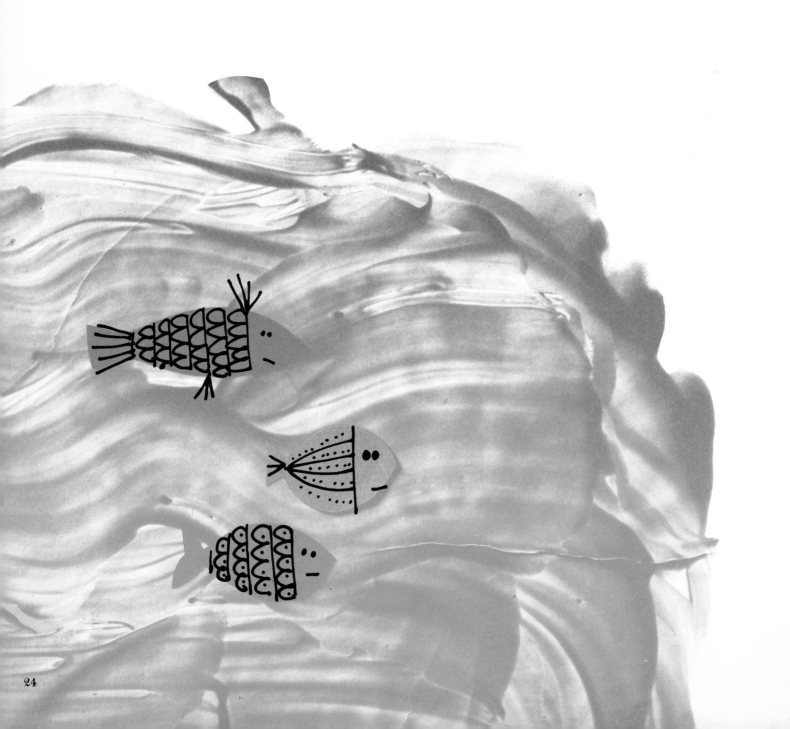

Very pleased and proud, the

No-Sort-of-Animal went skipping

off to the water hole.

But when he tried sucking up water

in his trunk like an elephant

the water came pouring out

of his ears in buckets.

And when he tried to make a

great trumpeting noise,

all that came out was

a very small

SQUEAK,

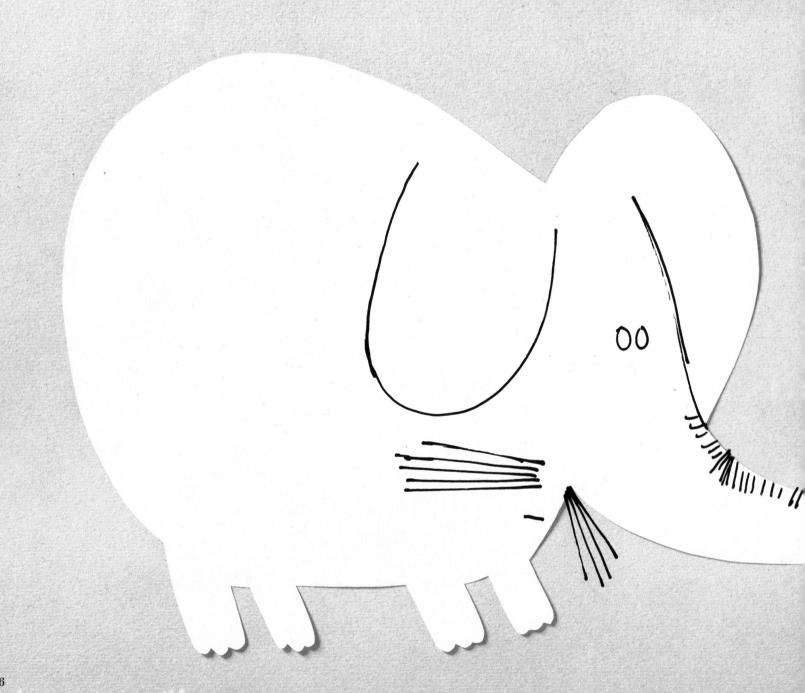

Which attracted the attention of a very small

mouse who came scampering up, looking worried.

"Are you all right?" the mouse asked.

"*Of course* I'm all right," the No-Sort-of-Animal said.

"Oh dear, you don't *look* it," the mouse said. "You

look very odd indeed. And besides you just made the

kind of noise that we mice make when we have a bad cold.

"Perhaps you should go home and wrap yourself up

in a blanket."

"Pooooooooooooofffff !!!!!"

said the No-Sort-of-Animal,
blowing so hard through
his trunk that he blew the
mouse right out of sight.

(Which was all the good he
got out of his trunk.
And not at all good enough.)

While he was sitting

feeling sad and

foolish, a hawk

came flying by.

He swooped down over

the No-Sort-of-Animal,

and then high

up into the sky.

"How handsome, how distinguished!" sighed the No-Sort-of-Animal.

Next day he went back to see the lion.

"Please," he said to the lion.

"I don't want an elephant's trunk
after all."

The lion was very cross.

"You do and you don't, and you
don't and you do!" he roared. "If you
don't want a giraffe's neck or an
elephant's trunk, what *do* you want?"

"Wings," said the No-Sort-of-Animal.

"You're an unpleasable sort of a
No-Sort-of-Animal," the lion grumbled.

But he arranged it anyway

LIKE

THIS

The No-Sort-of-Animal
was very pleased
and proud. Now he
would fly way above the
forest like the hawk.
It never occurred to
him that he really
wasn't built like a bird.
All he could do was to go
up

and up

and up

and up

and

after practicing

way up there

very, very

diligently

he began to

come

down

and

down

and

down

and

ka-splash!!!!!

into

the

water hole.

Very sadly, next day, the No-Sort-of-Animal

took his wings back to the lion.

"I guess it's no use," he said to the lion.

"I'll just have to stay a No-Sort-of-Animal

always, and a plain one at that."

"Now wait a minute," said the lion.

"I have been thinking things over.

You know you're really not a No-Sort-of-Animal

at all. You're really a perfectly good

sort of dog, as you will plainly see when

I give you this

TAIL!"

"A dog with a tail!"

exclaimed the dog

who used to be

a No-Sort-of-Animal.

"How handsome!

How distinguished!"

So he tried out his new tail.

He tried wagging it

and it wagged very well indeed.

He tried barking

and he barked very well indeed.

"What a handsome dog!"

the other dogs said.

"What a distinguished tail!"

"What a fine bark!"

"Thank you," said the dog

who used to be

a No-Sort-of-Animal

"Shall we all bark together?"

46

So they did. And then
they all ran and jumped
and played together until
it was time for everyone
to go home.
So off trotted the new
dog, *very* pleased and proud,
with his tail straight
up in the air, and he was
a dog ever after.

(For you know there are many, many dogs

who would be No-Sort-of-Animals if they

didn't happen to have tails.)